CW01583047

101 THINGS TO DO WHILE STUCK IN THE AIRPORT

Max Hultberg

Published by:
BAC BOOKS Publishing
TILL ALL THE NETS ARE FULL!
Division of BAC Ministries

Copyright © 2016 Max Hultberg

All rights reserved. No part of this publication may be reproduced, stored in a retrieval system or transmitted, in any form, or by any means, electronic, mechanical, recorded, photocopied, or otherwise, without the prior written permission of both the copyright owner and the above publisher of this book, except by a reviewer who may quote brief passages in a review.

The scanning, uploading, and distribution of this book via the Internet or via any other means without the permission of the publisher is illegal and punishable by law. Please purchase only authorized electronic editions and do not participate in or encourage electronic piracy of copyrightable mate-rials. Your support of the author's rights is appreciated.

Cover Image: airportrometransfer.com
Editorial snippets from the Evidence Bible

Dedicated to
My two best friends,
Jesus Christ and Michelle Hultberg (my wife).

1

HAVE courtesy wheelchair race with strangers.

2

PRETEND to be late for your flight and run full speed to your gate.

3

HAVE random people paged to the baggage claim.

4

VOLUNTEER to work the TSA Check Point.

5

ASK the ticket counter how much it is to ride the baggage check conveyer belt.

6

CHALLENGE a stranger to a thumb war.

7

TAKE a long ride on the baggage claim carousel.

8

COLLECT luggage carts and return for spare change.

9

GO to every gate counter and beg for peanuts.

10

CHALLENGE those around you to a game of paper, scissors, rock.

11

GO to the gate counter and complain when your flight is actually on time.

12

WALK backwards on the escalators.

13

RUN full speed on the moving walkways.

14

PULL cash from the ATM and yell "I won, I finally won!"

15

WHILE in the full body scanner scream, "Make it stop, it burns!"

16

LEAVE your bags unattended and see what happens – NEVER MIND, BAD IDEA!

17

GO to the nearest shop and rave about the low prices especially for $5.00 waters.

18

WALK through the metal detectors and make a “BEEP” sound.

19

ASK the attendants at the desk if you can be upgraded to first class for free.

20

HELP people collect their belongings at the security check.

21

ASK to be downgraded from coach.

22

FIND an outlet and plug in as many devices as possible.

23

TRY to become a "Barter King" at your gate.

24

SEE how many times you can go through the security check point before someone recognizes you.

25

SLOW motion run to your gate.

26

PUT your sunglasses (or glasses) on you head and in a frenzy illicit the help of everyone around to help find them.

27

ASK people near you if you could have a bite of whatever they are eating (even if you already have something you are eating).

28

START a push up contest.

29

FIND a busy shop and read a book....out loud!

30

ASK a smoker, “since I don’t smoke, could I just bum $5 from you instead?”

31

START that novel you always wanted to write.

32

PURPOSELY find people wearing headphones to strike up conversations with.

33

TAKE luggage off of the carousel and make a fort.

34

START a neck pillow fight.

35

TAKE a survey of everyone at your gate and where they are going.

36

GO to the currency exchange office and ask what the going rate of the US dollar is compared to the Federal Reserve Note..

37

TAKE the train/shuttle around the whole airport....multiple times.

38

OBTAIN a pair of pilot wings and make sure to wear them proudly (the older you are the better).

39

GO to the rental car desk and inquire how much it would cost to rent a vehicle to drive around the airport in circles while you wait for your flight.

40

STAND facing the jetway and make silly faces at the workers.

41

HOLD a paper airplane contest at your gate.

42

STAND by baggage claim holding a paper with a common last name (example: Smith). When someone comes up, see how far they will follow you.

43

GO to the information desk and ask for information on random trivia. Example: What are the average eating habits of a Tibetan Yak in winter verses the summer months?

44

START a petition to increase wait times at airports and try to obtain signatures.

45

SEE how many complimentary baggage tags can fit on one piece of luggage. Make sure they are filled out in entirety.

46

FIND the welcome desk and stand there until you get "welcome."

47

HAVE your gate challenge the gate across the terminal to a game of Red Rover.

48

HUNT for the most obnoxious souvenir.

49

RACE the people on the moving walkways.

50

VISIT the Lost Luggage desk and inquire if you can have any unclaimed luggage.

EDITORIAL: Have you ever flown in a plane? Sitting in a window seat is a neat experience, especially at night. As you ascend into the air, the city below gets smaller and smaller. Soon the buildings that once towered high above your head now look like Legos. Highways appear as small paths among a sea of lights. But as I look down from thousands of feet high above the earth, I start to ponder about Psalm 8. What is man that God would even notice or pay us any mind? I can tell you, from this vantage point, I find it extremely hard to think of the nameless thousands below. But that is not the case with God, strangely enough, He not only considers everyone, but knows them by name, and loves them enough to die for them. But don't let me get ahead of myself.

It is true God made us, and in His image by the way, how amazing is that? We are all made in the very image of our Creator. That in and of itself gives us automatic and unprecedented worth. You don't need to do any-thing to be valuable, you already are valuable. It is also true that based on this worth, God made us to be over His creation and to moreover to have dominion over it (Genesis 1:28; Psalm 8:5-8). Man is made to be intellectually superior to rest of creation and has priority over it - every animal is under his feet and may be brought submission by him (James 3:7). Think about that for a moment:

Birds (parrots) can be taught to speak. With a crack of a whip lions will do what he says. Even killer whales obey his voice. Cows yield milk for his cereal, cheese for his pizza, butter for his bread, yogurt to keep him healthy, and ice cream to delight his taste buds on hot days. The same cow gives him meat to keep him strong and leather to keep him warm. Sheep and goats also yield many of these same products. The chicken makes eggs for his breakfast and provides finger-licking meat for his dinner. The sea overflows with an incredible variety of fish for him to catch and eat. Dogs protect his property and herd his sheep. Elephants lift great weights for him. Camels carry him across deserts. The horse is perfectly designed to be ridden by him. Man's God given dominion is obvious.

God who is also omniscient (all knowing), knows every one of us by name. He knows how many hairs we have on our heads (Matthew 10:30), and for some that is easier to count than others. He also knows the stars by name (Psalm 147:4, Isaiah 40:26). The stars by name! Do you know how many stars there are? Recent estimates of the known universe (and that isn't even the part we haven't seen yet) state there are ten billion trillion stars, putting that in perspective that means that each individual on earth today could personally have a trillion stars to themselves. So what about the Love of God, where does that come into play? The Bible clearly states that God is love (1 John 4:8), but we need to consider the depth of that love and how that love is manifested toward us. Let me explain: Probably the most well-known verse in the Bible is John 3:16, for God so love the world.... But what many fail to realize is that there is more to that verse, which not only demonstrates God's love but His holiness, goodness, wrath, and justice as well.

God demonstrated His love toward us in that while we were still sinners Christ died for us (Romans 5:8).
A study of the New Testament will show almost always God's love in direct correlation to the cross (See John 3:16; Romans 5:6,7,8; Galatians 2:20; Ephesians 2:4,5; 5:2,25; 1John 3:16; 4:10; and Revelation 1:5, among others). The cross is the focal point of God's love for the world. You see God's love is directly proportionate to His

justice. If God is absolute love then He is absolute just as well.
He spared not His Son, the infinite punishment laid on Him, was the fullness of God's wrath that was meant for us - this is the ultimate demonstration of love.

But! This amazing act of love and ultimate sacrifice will only make sense if you or I see ourselves as sinners.
So let's take a few moments to make sure we have a good grasp on this truth, the difference can be eternally significant. In God's infinite wisdom, He made a sure fire way to know if you are good enough to get to heaven or bad enough to deserve hell, and the answer may surprise you.
Do you think you have kept the Ten Commandments? Let's take a quick test and see how you do.

[9th] Have you ever told a lie (including white lies, half-truths, and exaggerations, etc)? If you have then you are a liar, and all liars will have their part in the lake of fire (Revelation 21:8).

[8th] Have you ever stolen (the value of the item is irrelevant)? Then you are a thief.

[7th] Jesus said that if you look with lust, you have committed adultery in your heart.

[6th] If you hate someone, then you have

committed murder in your heart. You see God requires truth in the inward parts (Psalms 51:6) - He sees even our thought-life. The eyes of the Lord are in every place, beholding the evil and the good (Proverbs 15:3). The God who made the eyes can see everything!

[1st] Have you loved God above all else? Has He always been first in your affections?

[2nd] Have you made a "god" to suit yourself (having your own beliefs about God)? That is called idolatry, and the Bible warns that no idolater will enter the kingdom of God.

[3rd] Have you ever used God's holy name to curse, [10th] or been greedy?

[4th] Have you kept the Sabbath holy? [5th] Have you always implicitly honored your parents?

Have you broken any of the Ten Commandments? Now knowing that God has seen your thought-life and every deed done in darkness, will you be innocent or guilty on Judgment Day? Will you end up in heaven or hell? If you are now seeing yourself (perhaps for the first time as a sinner), wait because there is good news just around the corner.

God gave us the Ten Commandments as a

mirror to show us our true state. Where the natural man wants to justify himself as being good (Proverbs 20:6), the evidence is overwhelming and not in our favor - there is NONE that does good, no, not one (Psalm 14:3; Romans 3:10-18). In fact, we are all guilty (see your score from the Ten Commandment test). For ALL have sinned (Romans 3:23), and sin according to 1 John 3:4 is transgression (or the breaking) of the Law (Ten Commandments). What the Law does if used lawfully
(1 Timothy 1:8-10) is stops our mouths from justification and brings the knowledge of sin (Romans 3:19-20). This is a great place to be in because the law ultimately leads us to Christ like a schoolmaster (Galatians 3:24). And a schoolmaster's job is to bring knowledge. We need this knowledge so we can see ourselves in truth. Then we can fully under-stand that we are not in good standing with the Judge of the universe in fact He (God) is angry with the wicked every day (Psalm 7:11) and His wrath is abiding on us instead (John 3:36). But once you have come to this point your heart is prepared for the good news. So here it is:

The only thing you can do to be saved from God's wrath is to repent and put your faith in the Savior, Jesus Christ. When He died on the cross, He took the punishment for our sins. He, once and for all, stepped into the Courtroom and completely paid the fine for jus. Then, He rose from the dead, defeating death. If you want to be saved from God's wrath, confess and forsake your sins, put your faith in Jesus for your eternal salvation, and you will pass from death into life. Then read the Bible daily and obey what you read (see John 14:21). God will never let you down.

51

STAND by the Security Check Point and collect the waters and sodas that cannot be taken through.

52

STAND by a blank wall and pretend you are admiring a work of art. Stare at it as though you are contemplating the artist's style.

53

LIE down and attempt to take a nap in the middle of the busiest terminal.

54

STAND in front of the Arrival/Departure screens until someone asks if you need some help....wait however long it takes.

55

OBTAIN a box from one of the shops, they try to sled down the escalators.

56

REARRANGE the seating at your gate.

57

ASK vendors selling cigarettes if they sell any that are "Gluten Free." Have them check every box to make sure.

58

STAND outside the restroom entrance and see how many people line up behind you.

59

ADMIRE someone's shoes and see if they will make a trade.

60

ASK the cahier at the Duty Free shop, "Why do I still have to pay if it is Duty FREE?"

61

PURCHASE a sandwich, eat 80% of it and then attempt to do a return or exchange.

62

GO to the restroom and get a long piece of toilet paper and tuck some into your shoe, then walk through the airport until someone stops you.

63

ASK random people for their autograph and to pose for a selfie with you.

64

CALL and have yourself paged to your gate for a complimentary First Class upgrade.

65

AFTER drinking a bottle of soda, go back to the shop it was purchased from and ask for a free refill.

66

HOLD up a cardboard sign at your gate reading "First Class or Bust."

67

PRACTICE your Hacky Sack skills. If you don't have a Hacky Sack, improvise by taking off one of your socks and rolling it up into a ball.

68

STRIKE up a conversation with a complete stranger but lead the conversation like you have known them for years.

69

ASK people for spare change for the ATM.

70

FIND a busy gate with no attendants and stand next to the podium, feel free to answer any questions that come your way.

71

TAKE an "Army Bath" in the sink in the restroom, the more crowded the better. Sing some shower tunes while you bath for added fun.

72

VISIT the health food counter and order a non-organic spring salad with extra pesticides on the side.

73

GO to Starbucks and order the Hawkins special: Grande Soy Cinnamon No-Foam Half-Calf Half-Sweet Extra Shot Extra Hot Three Pump Vanilla Upside-Down Carmel Macchiato Double Sleeve No Cup.

74

START a "Dance Off" using only Hip Hop moves from the 80's/90's.

75

GET on the floor and crawl around like you are looking for one of your contacts (even better if you don't wear any).

76

ASK the gate attendant since you might feel Claustrophobic while sitting in Coach, if they think it was better if you were upgraded to First Class.

77

ASK a bartender at one of the airport bars if they serve non-alcoholic liquor.

78

FIND a partner and play wheelchair chick (Don't let them win).

79

PRACTICE your handstands (if you have no clue how to do it, even better).

80

PRETEND you are a Secret Agent and use random things in your bag to set up surveillance on someone at your gate.

81

FIND the guy with the biggest muscles and ask if he ever thought about going to the gym once in a while.

82

GO to one of the shops and say, "I am with the North American Candy Quality Control Division, the NACQC, and am conduction an inspection. I will need to confiscate any W's that may be found in your bags of M&M's."

83

WAIT for an airport police officer to get close and then jump up and take off running.

Never mind, probably not a good idea!

84

ASK airport personnel to help you find someone you are traveling with: giver them your exact description.

85

GO to a restaurant and order a "Diet Water" with your meal.

86

OBTAIN color pages and crayons from one of the airlines. Color several pages and then set up an art show to display and sell your works of art.

87

USE your cell phone to make a pretend call to airport security, alert them of suspicious activity and give them the description of the individual sitting right next to you.

88

WALK up and down the terminal borrowing pens from people: see how many you can collect.

89

ORDER a pizza from Dominos and see if they will deliver to your gate.

90

GET your Congress man or woman on the phone and have a heart to heart talk about getting back to the "Gold Standard."

91

WALK around your gate tapping people on the head saying, "duck, duck....goose."

92

GO to another gate and see if someone wants to trade flights.

93

START a flag football game airline against airline. Use socks as the flags and your shoe as the football.

94

START your obsession with Angry Birds all over again.

95

LEARN to speak a foreign language.

96

START a Hopscotch tournament.

97

BALANCE your checkbook; then offer to balance those at your gate as well.

98

LEARN to read Braille.

99

CALL the airline and ask how much it would be to check a hippopotamus, mention that is all your daughter wants for Christmas, well that and her two front teeth.

100

ASK the cashier at a news stand if they have tomorrow's paper because today's is already yesterday's news.

101

READ this book and don't forget to read the editorial!

Thank you for reading this book!

Don't forget to check out Max Hultberg's other books:

101 of the World's Dumbest Criminals

Criminals have never been mistaken for brain surgeons, or rocket scientists for that matter, and this book will show you the reason why. See the greatest collection of stories about the dumbest criminals in all their glory. Make sure and see who takes the cake and is awarded the title as the World's Dumbest Criminal.

Drive Fast & Take Chances

Things Other Drivers Do To Annoy You

Have you ever felt your blood pressure rise as you get behind the wheel or end up in a rage by the time you get to your destination? Hopefully this book will help drop those nerves down a couple thousand RPMs. Enjoy a comical look at the wide range of things that other drivers do to annoy each and everyone of us.

Printed in Dunstable, United Kingdom

63592430R00068